COMING HOME

This book is dedicated to the mothers and fathers
who put themselves in harm's way for the sake
of their families—and ours.

A Feiwel and Friends Book
An Imprint of Macmillan

COMING HOME. Copyright © 2014 by Greg Ruth. All rights reserved. Printed in China by South China Printing Co. Ltd., Dongguan City, Guangdong Province. For information, address Feiwel and Friends, 175 Fifth Avenue, New York, N.Y. 10010.

Feiwel and Friends books may be purchased for business or promotional use. For information on bulk purchases, please contact the Macmillan Corporate and Premium Sales Department at (800) 221-7945 x5442 or by e-mail at specialmarkets@macmillan.com.

Library of Congress Cataloging-in-Publication Data Available

ISBN: 978-1-250-05547-7

Book design by Ashley Halsey

Feiwel and Friends logo designed by Filomena Tuosto

First Edition: 2014

10 9 8 7 6 5 4 3 2 1

mackids.com

Greg Ruth

COMING HOME

FEIWEL AND FRIENDS

NEW YORK

Waiting.

Watching.

Go!

Lucky dog.

Where is . . . ?

Sheesh!

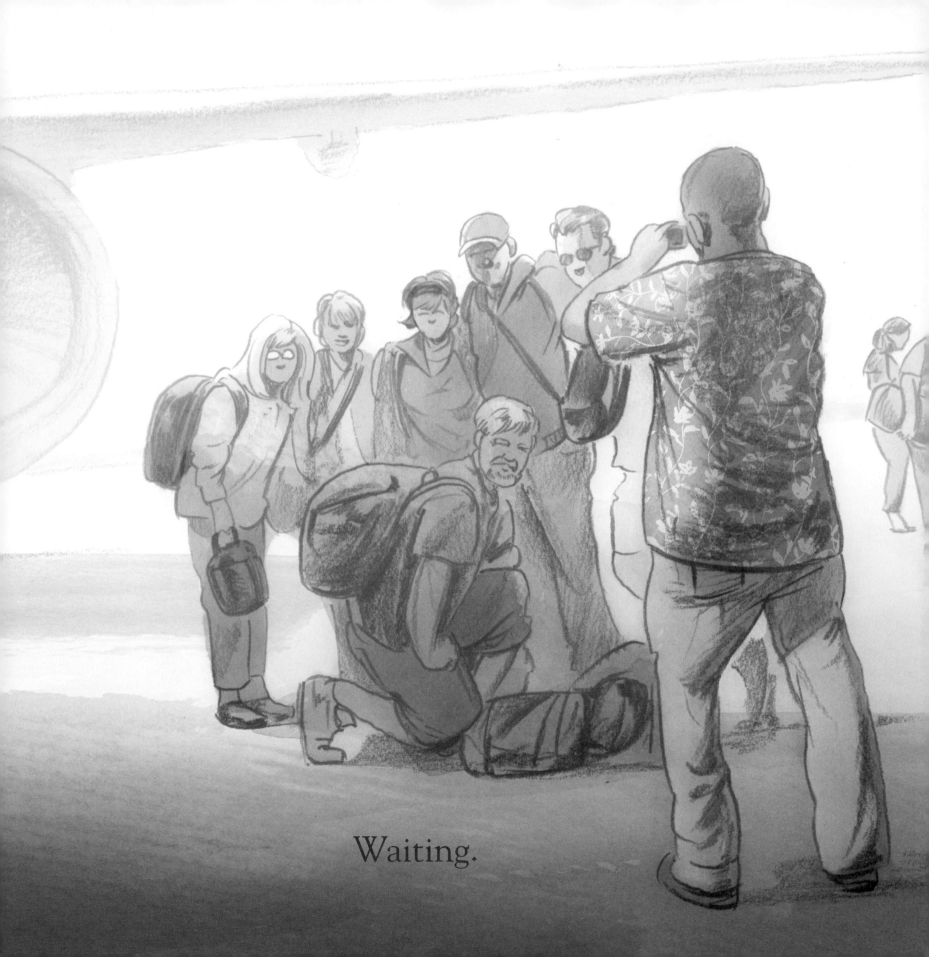

Waiting.

Watching.

Where is . . . ?

MOM!

I missed you *so* much.

Author's Note

Making this book has been a deeply surprising and rewarding enterprise. I've spent a great deal of time researching reunion videos and stories of returning soldiers online, and have seen how often the effect of this side of the military experience is absent from our conversation about war. No soldier goes to war alone—he or she always brings along their family and friends with them. In the service of such a unique and often hidden experience of going to war, I felt getting this right was the most important way to honor those fortunate enough to come home to the loving arms of those whom they have left behind.

Crafting a (mostly) wordless children's picture book about such a profound experience is challenging in many ways. There's a lot of mechanical planning that goes into mapping out something like this, but the ultimate test is how it feels to read it. You plan and build and trust that the sum of all its parts comes together into something larger. It's like sculpting in the dark and then turning on the light when you're done to see what you've made and decide if it's working. I hope this book works for you. —Greg Ruth